D0370404

I couldn't laugh it off.

"Don't worry about it, Jodi," said Lauren. "Nobody's blaming you because we lost."

The very fact that Lauren would say that seemed to me to mean my teammates *were* blaming me.

"Nobody can accuse Jodi of worrying too much, right?" joked Cindi.

"It's a proven fact that people who don't worry live longer," answered Lauren.

"But do they make better gymnasts?" I wondered out loud.

Lauren giggled. "That's funny."

I bit my lip. Cindi and Lauren were my two best friends on the team, but I didn't like them teasing me about not worrying. It made me feel like an airhead.

**Look for these and other books
in THE GYMNASTS series:**

THE GYMNASTS

#21 TEAM TROUBLE

Elizabeth Levy

AN
APPLE
PAPERBACK

SCHOLASTIC INC.
New York Toronto London Auckland Sydney

If you purchased this book without a cover, you should be aware that this book is stolen property. It was reported as "unsold and destroyed" to the publisher, and neither the author nor the publisher has received any payment for this "stripped book."

No part of this publication may be reproduced in whole or in part, or stored in a retrieval system, or transmitted in any form or by any means, electronic, mechanical, photocopying, recording, or otherwise, without written permission of the publisher. For information regarding permission, write to Scholastic Inc., 730 Broadway, New York, NY 10003.

ISBN 0-590-45252-5

Copyright © 1992 by Elizabeth Levy
All rights reserved. Published by Scholastic Inc.
APPLE PAPERBACKS is a registered trademark of Scholastic Inc.
THE GYMNASTS is a trademark of Scholastic Inc.

12 11 10 9 8 7 6 5 4 3 2 1   2 3 4 5 6 7/9

Printed in the U.S.A.   28

First Scholastic printing, February 1992

To the Sqlzberg Speedsters

Dump the Slump

"Today I'm going to dump the slump!" I said to my teammates, the Pinecones. I was in a good mood even though I was having a lousy day. If there's one thing I know it's that you can't win them all. Lately I hadn't been able to win *any* of them.

"That a girl, Jodi, dump the slump! Dump the slump!" the Pinecones started chanting.

I walked over to the chalk bin. When I leaned over it to get chalk on my hands for a better grip on the bars, I bent over too far. My long blonde hair, which I had pulled over to one side, dipped into the chalk first. Great. I couldn't even do the chalk bin right.

"Go, Jodi!" shouted my teammates from the

bench, but they didn't sound as if their hearts were in it. Lauren Baca was fiddling with her leotard. Darlene Broderick was checking her latest hairdo. Her thick black hair was pulled back with a green-and-white band that matched our leotards.

Cindi Jockett studied the pattern on the floor. Ti An Truong nervously licked her lips, and Ashley Frank looked as if she were counting the light bulbs on the ceiling.

Nobody was looking at me. It was as if I were a walking disaster area, and everybody was afraid that what I had was catching.

I was not having a good day — or a good week or even a good month, for that matter. I knew it. My coach, Patrick, knew it, and now the opposing team and the judges knew it.

We were at a meet with our archrivals, the Atomic Amazons. January through March was our meet season, but so far all that I had been meeting was disaster. This was our second meet of the season. I had already goofed up my vault and my beam routine. Now I had bars. Normally it's my best event. I'm the second best on my team. I always go right before Cindi, who's the best. Ti An Truong is moving up. But bars is *my* event. I have always loved to fly. Patrick saves the best for the last, because that's what the judges expect.

Patrick came up to give me some last-minute advice. "I know, I know," I said quickly, predicting what he would say. "Turn the page. I had a lousy beam, but forget it. It's a brand-new slate."

"It's not a cliché, Jodi," said Patrick. "In gymnastics, every event is a chance for a new page. That's the way you've got to think of it."

I wish I had a dollar for every time Patrick's told one of us to turn the page. I'd never have to worry about money.

I clapped my hands together, setting off a cloud of chalk.

"Concentrate on your giant circle. It's been giving you trouble in practice lately," said Patrick, ducking to avoid my dust storm.

"What *hasn't* been giving me trouble?" I joked.

"Just stay focused," said Patrick. "Try to stay in the moment. Concentrate on exactly what you have to do now. Don't let yourself get distracted."

"Right. Dump the slump," I said.

"Jodi, everybody goes through a lull now and then. The trick is not to let it play mind games with your gymnastics. Break each event into a bunch of little tasks."

I rolled my eyes. For two minutes, I'd be swinging from one bar five feet off the ground to another bar seven-and-a-half feet above the ground. I'd get points off every time I bent my elbows or forgot to point my toes. That not my idea of an easy task.

I dipped my hands into the chalk bin one last time. When I'm nervous I practically take a bath in the chalk dust. I shook my hands and shrugged my shoulders.

"What have I got to lose?" I said to Patrick.

He didn't laugh.

"It's only my life, right?" I muttered.

"Enough with the jokes, Jodi," said Patrick. He patted me on the shoulder, trying to give me confidence.

The head judge was an ash-blonde woman in her forties. So many of the judges look as if they wake up in the morning with every hair in place. This judge seemed to be looking at me as if I could use Dustbusting. I looked down at myself. I had white blobs of chalk dust on my thighs.

I saluted the judge with my right hand and tried to rub off the chalk dust with my left. Not exactly the best way to make a good impression.

I shrugged as I walked to the center of the mats. My eyes were about level with the lower bar. I remember when I was little and my mom would have to lift me to the low bar. It seemed like it was miles above my head. My mom and dad met while they were both doing gymnastics. Mom was better than Dad. She was on our national team. Mom and Dad have been divorced for a long time, though. My sister, Jennifer, is at the Air Force Academy. She's a great gymnast. She takes after Mom.

I shook my head. I was in the middle of a meet. This was no time for negative thoughts.

My approach to the bars is an easy one. I just grab the lower bar and slide under it, kicking my legs up and bending my body. Patrick always tells us to pretend we're trying to put on a pair of pajama bottoms with our toes. It's called a glide kip, and even beginners use it to swing up onto the bar.

Only today, instead of a glide kip, I did a glide kip-buttle. I just lost control of the bar. It slipped out of my hands, and the next thing I knew I fell hard on my butt.

I was down for the count before I began. I heard somebody giggle behind me. I figured it had to be one of the Atomic Amazons laughing at me.

It wasn't. It was Becky Dyson, a girl from my own gym. She's on the more advanced team, the Needles. Becky is the meanest girl in our gym, but she *is* supposed to be on my side.

I looked over at the Pinecones. They looked genuinely distressed. Lauren gave Becky a dirty look.

I had only a few seconds left in which to get back on the bars or I'd be disqualified. I'm not a quitter. I grabbed the bar and went through my routine. I didn't fall again, but I was sloppy.

I didn't even wait for my score. I knew it would be bad. I went back to the bench and sat down. "Sorry, guys," I said.

Nobody said anything. They didn't have to. I knew I had let them down. Even if Cindi did exceptionally well on the bars, there was no way that we weren't going to lose. I had seen to that.

I got up and spread my arms wide and shrugged and grinned. At least I could laugh at myself. I might be having a disastrous day, but there was no need to lose my sense of humor. Or was there?

What If the Book Is Lousy?

The Atomic Amazons have the most swanky locker rooms. They share their facilities with a health club in a fancy downtown Denver hotel, and every part of the locker room glows pink. There is a pink carpet and soft pink lighting. Even the benches are upholstered in pink.

"Did anyone notice that I clash?" I asked as we went into the locker room to change back into our street clothes.

Cindi stared at me. "What do you mean?" she asked. "I'm the one with red hair. I clash."

"Right," said Darlene. "Blondes look good in pink."

"Yeah, but I'm a red-hot loser," I said. "Red-hot losers should not have to look at themselves in pink mirrors. On the other hand, maybe you can't tell I'm a loser when I'm in the pink."

"You're not a loser," said Darlene automatically. She plopped down on the upholstered bench. She looked bushed. She took off her headband. "What a way to start the meet season," she said with a sigh. "We didn't even win one event."

Becky came in dangling a medal from around her neck. She was carrying a big trophy and a bunch of flowers. Becky's team had won the all-around.

She elbowed me aside and put her trophy on the mirrored vanity. It glowed in the pink light.

"Don't touch it," she warned me. "I don't want you to bring me bad luck."

I felt myself turning red. Now I did truly clash with all that pink. "Sorry," I mumbled. I couldn't even think of a comeback.

Lauren came to my defense. "Hey, Becky," she shouted, rousing herself from the bench. "Knock it off. Jodi had a hard enough day without you riding her."

Becky blinked. "Did I insult you?" she asked me. "I was just teasing. I never thought you took anything seriously."

"Becky," I said, "thanks for the compliment." I was being sarcastic.

"Well, I meant it as a compliment," said Becky defensively. "I thought you didn't mind losing."

"Becky!" I gasped. I couldn't believe that she would really think that losing didn't hurt.

"I mean it," said Becky. "You're so loosey-goosey, I figured it rolls off your back."

"Yeah, right," I said. "That's me, old loose as a goose."

"There's such a thing as being too loose," said Heidi Ferguson.

Heidi had just walked into the locker room. Heidi doesn't compete in our meets. If she did, the entire Atomic Amazon team would be wiped out by her scores. There is almost nobody in the entire Denver area that can give Heidi competition. She is one of the best gymnasts in the entire country, if not the world. She performs exhibition meets in Denver, and then she competes around the world at different international challenge meets. She is almost sure to be on the American team for the Olympics this summer — she is *that* good.

The weirdest thing about Heidi is that she still gets a kick out of the Pinecones. Unlike Becky, Heidi actually thinks of all of us as her good-luck charm.

Heidi looks a little funny in street clothes, as if she should always be wearing a leotard. She's thin with short black hair and big dark eyes. She's small. She's shorter than I am. She's almost fifteen. Except for when she's performing, she doesn't like to wear makeup, so she looks even younger.

I admire Heidi, but I'm always a little awkward around her. She is so focused and sure of herself in gymnastics. She's tough. She's not nasty like Becky, but she's got a kind of brutal honesty. And she doesn't have much of a sense of humor.

"Look, Heidi," I said, "I know I didn't do well today, okay?"

"Turn the page," said Cindi. "That's all you can do."

"Slumps are awful," said Darlene. "Everybody's been in one of them. My dad says you just can't let yourself get psyched out about it." Darlene's dad is "Big Beef" Broderick. He's an offensive lineman for the Denver Broncos, and they certainly had a lousy season last year.

"Patrick says 'turn the page,' " repeated Cindi. "That's all Jodi has to do. Isn't that right, Heidi?"

Heidi didn't answer.

"Heidi?" repeated Cindi.

"I'm lousy at giving advice to other people," muttered Heidi.

"But Patrick always tells us to turn the page," insisted Lauren. "It's the only thing you can do."

All the Pinecones nodded their heads as if those were magic words of Patrick's that would make everything all right. Everybody except Heidi.

10

"What if it's a lousy book?" I said.

The Pinecones all laughed as if I were making a terrific joke. Heidi didn't laugh. I think that she understood as well as I did that it didn't help to turn the page if the book stunk.

3

What? Me Worry?

Mom picked me up at school with my baby brother, Travis, strapped into the backseat. Travis is my half brother. I've got a whole new family. My stepfather is Barney Josephson. He runs a string of pet stores in the Denver area called Barking Barney's.

Everybody knows Barking Barney. His ads are on the radio all the time. They always start with a dumb riddle about an animal. I used to be terribly embarrassed that my mom was dating the actual Barking Barney, but then I found out that almost all my friends love his ads. I don't mind being teased about being related to Barking Barney, although I get a little tired of hearing everybody's favorite stupid animal joke.

The real problem is that Barking Barney came with a son from his first marriage, Nick the Pest. Maybe I could blame my slump on Nick. The only advantage to having Nick around is that I now have somebody to blame when things go wrong.

It was Monday, and Mom was giving me, Lauren, and Cindi a ride to the gym. Mom's started working again at the Evergreen Gymnastics Academy. She no longer coaches the boys' team full time, but she's in charge of the tiny tots program. Back in St. Louis my mom and my real dad used to own their own gymnastics school. Dad still runs it. He's a very strict coach, and he almost always has winning teams. I was glad that he wasn't around to see the way my team was losing.

I don't think Mom likes the fact that I'm in a slump, either. In Mom's day, she was a killer competitor. Of course, even she admits she couldn't do half the stuff that Heidi now does routinely. That's how much gymnastics has changed in the past couple of decades.

Travis gave me a grin. When he smiles, it's lopsided but cute. I like it when he smiles at me. It makes me feel good.

I got into the backseat beside him. "I'll sit with Travis," I said. "Ol' Trav, here, doesn't mind sitting next to a loser." Cindi got into the front seat next to my mom, and Lauren piled in next to me.

Mom turned around in her seat. "Jodi," she said, "I don't like you calling yourself a loser."

"Neither do we," said Cindi. She looked at my mom earnestly. I like Cindi, but sometimes she can be a little bit of a goody-goody. She's gotten real close to my mom ever since she started to work with her in the tiny tots program. Cindi's dad is still out of work, and Cindi helps pay for her gymnastics lessons by helping Mom and Patrick with the little kids.

Travis waved his hand above the bar of his car seat, but he kept hitting his hand on the bar. I've been trying to teach him to give me a high five, but Travis doesn't have it all together yet.

I gave his little hand a pat. "Put it there, partner," I said, taking his hand and showing him how to slide his palm across mine.

"We've been telling Jodi to put last weekend's meet behind her," said Lauren.

"If anybody else tells me to turn the page, I'll scream," I warned them.

"You have another meet in a few weeks," said Mom. "You'll do better then."

"Right, Jodi," said Lauren. "Don't worry about it. Nobody's blaming you for the fact that we lost."

I crossed my eyes. The very fact that Lauren would say that seemed to me to mean my teammates *were* blaming me.

"Yeah," joked Cindi. "Nobody can accuse Jodi of worrying too much. Isn't that right, Mrs. Josephson?"

"Sarah," said Mom. "Cindi, you can call me Sarah. Remember?"

I still couldn't get used to my mom being called Mrs. Josephson. My last name is Sutton. It's my dad's name.

"It's a proven fact that people who don't worry live longer," said Lauren.

"Yeah, but do they make better gymnasts?" I wondered out loud.

"Very funny," said Lauren. She giggled.

I bit my lip. Cindi and Lauren were my two best friends on the team, but I didn't like them teasing me about not worrying. It made me feel like an airhead.

When we got to the gym, Heidi was already hard at work. I stopped to watch her. I get a real kick out of watching Heidi. She was working on her new floor routine with Dimitri Vickorskoff, the famous Hungarian coach. Dimitri came to this country with no money and ended up sleeping in our gym when Patrick gave him a job. But now, with the Olympics only a few months away, Dimitri and Heidi are getting a lot of attention. Every few weeks, it seems, we have TV reporters coming to our little gym to record Heidi's progress.

Heidi is an incredibly powerful gymnast. When she's standing still, she doesn't look that commanding, but when she's on the mats, she takes over the whole space.

Dimitri was counting out the rhythm as she practiced her first tumbling pass. "Von, two, three, vour!" he shouted. Heidi raised her hands over her head and then threw herself high in the air. She crossed her arms over her chest, keeping her body straight as a board, as she whipped through the air, nearly ten feet above the mats, doing a double layout, which is mainly a men's tumbling skill on the floor exercise. Not many women compete with a double layout. Mary Lou Retton was the very first.

Heidi finished the double layout with a huge lunge.

"No! No!" yelled Dimitri. "All wrong." It had looked perfect to me.

"Your wrists, your wrists, and your elbows! They bulge out!" shouted Dimitri. "No, no. They must be close to your body, like this." Dimitri hugged himself.

"Now, von more time!"

Heidi was still out of breath. She was doubled over with her hands on her knees, gulping for air.

She nodded her head, agreeing with Dimitri.

Then she straightened up and went to the edge of the mat to do it again.

"Wow!" said Ti An, coming to stand beside me. Ti An had already changed into her leotard.

"Double wow!" I admitted.

"I'd better get started warming up," said Ti An.

I looked at my watch. We still had fifteen minutes before our class officially began. I hadn't even changed out of my street clothes.

Ti An went over to the bar and began her stretches. She's only nine, and she's incredibly flexible. I used to be like her. I could do a perfect one-hundred-and-eighty-degree split without even thinking about it. Now that I'm eleven, almost twelve, I'm just not as flexible as I used to be.

I looked around. Darlene, Cindi, Lauren, and Ashley had already changed. I hurried across the gym to the locker room. Patrick, with a clipboard in his hand, was talking to my mom. He looked around the gym and saw that all the other Pinecones were already dressed for gymnastics and warming up.

"Get a move on, Jodi," he warned me.

"I'm on time," I argued. "The others are just early."

"No excuses," said Mom. "Just shake a leg."

I rolled my eyes. Mom and I had made a deal

very early on. She would never be my coach. So it wasn't Mom's job to tell me to get moving. Besides, I was in the right. The other kids were early. I still had ten minutes.

I pushed open the door into the locker room. Becky was just changing into her leotard. Her team started their workouts half an hour after we did.

"Running late?" Becky asked me.

"I was just watching Heidi," I snapped. "I was here in plenty of time."

Becky raised one eyebrow. She has a knack of doing it.

"Touchy, touchy, aren't we?" said Becky.

"No," I said distinctly. "I am not touchy. I am just here on time."

"Sure, sure," said Becky. "Why worry? You're the original what-me-worry girl, right?"

I glared at her. It was the second time in one day that I had been told that I wasn't the worrying kind. It was beginning to worry me.

Vot's Best
for the Pinecones —
Rotten for Me

I changed into my tights and T-shirt as quickly as I could and rushed out to the gym. I glanced up at the clock. I *was* just on time, but my teammates were practically finished with their warm-ups. It wasn't fair.

I tried not to hurry my stretches. I've seen too many gymnasts hurt themselves because they were in a rush. I still had a few exercises to do when Patrick blew his whistle for us to gather around the bars.

"Finish your stretches, Jodi," said Patrick. "Join us when you're ready."

I was doing a split. I looked up at him. Patrick is almost never sarcastic, but I didn't like the

19

sound of "Join us when you're ready." I couldn't read his face.

I shrugged and struggled to stretch out just a little further. I could feel the muscles in my hamstrings pull out as I lifted myself into a long lunge and then stretched out my calf muscles.

I finally finished my warm-ups and jogged over to the bars. Darlene gave me a smile.

"Patrick's got a new trick up his sleeve," she whispered to me.

"This new move isn't for everybody," said Patrick. "All of you won't use it in the meets this year, but some of you might catch on to it. It's a high-level skill, but it's one of those tricks that looks harder than it is. Most of you have already mastered the basics."

I was totally lost. It was like being in school after being out sick and having no idea what the subject was. What basics?

"What's he talking about?" I whispered to Darlene.

"A new release move from the high bar," Darlene whispered back.

"Darlene and Jodi," said Patrick, "pay attention, here. Jodi, you're one of the girls who I think should be able to do this new move with ease."

"I'm sorry I'm late," I mumbled, although I knew that I *wasn't* late.

"It's okay," said Patrick. "We started a few minutes early. It wasn't your fault."

I breathed a sigh of relief. Patrick is fair. That's what I like the most about him.

"Okay," I said, rubbing my hands together. "Tell me about this release move! Maybe I can wipe out the Atomic Amazons with it. I'd like to release them from the universe."

Ti An laughed, "Me, too," she said.

Patrick went to the chalkboard and drew a diagram of the move. "You start with a giant backward circle, the way you've been doing it," he said. "Then at the top of the circle, you release the bar, cross your hands, and do a one-hundred-and-eighty-degree turn. The twist is almost foolproof. You already have the momentum, the only trick is the timing of crossing and uncrossing your hands."

"Foolproof," I joked. "Well, I'm the perfect fool, so if it can be proofed against me, anybody can do it."

"You're not the perfect fool," said Patrick.

I grinned at him. "Well, nobody's perfect," I said. It was something that Patrick had taught me long ago.

"Letting go of the bar when you're falling backward," shuddered Lauren. "This move is not for me."

Lauren is almost fearless. She'll do anything

Patrick tells her to so long as it's going forward. She's an incredible vaulter, because in a vault, even if she's doing a back handstand, her momentum is always forward.

Lauren says it's a natural instinct for humans not to want to fall back. I must be a freak of nature then, because it's never bothered me.

"Come on, Ti An," said Patrick. "You try it first."

I frowned. Normally Cindi or I would be the first person to try it.

Ti An chalked up. Patrick held her up to put extra chalk on the high bar so that her hands wouldn't slip when she went to regrab it. Ti An did it carefully. I was getting impatient. I couldn't wait to try the new move myself.

Finally Ti An was satisfied that the bar had enough chalk on it. She took hold of the lower bar. She's so tiny, she's about six inches shorter than I am, and she whips around the bars quickly. Everything Ti An does looks as if it doesn't require any effort.

Patrick stood under the bars ready to spot Ti An if she needed it. "Good, Ti An, good," he said. She started to swing into her backward circle. A backward circle around the high bar has always been hard for Ti An because she's a teensy bit scared of falling back, a little like Lauren.

I watched to see how Ti An was going to do when it came time for her to let go of the bar. She was falling backward, having circled the high bar, but she didn't look good. Her toes weren't pointed, and her arms were bent at the elbows. At the top of the bar, she quickly shuffled her hands. She didn't really have much height over the bar, but she managed to catch it again. Patrick put up his arms to steady her.

"Good, good," he said. He helped Ti An lower to the mats. Ti An was flushed. She looked scared. Her chest was going in and out.

"It *is* scary," she said.

"But you did it!" said Patrick, patting her on the back. "The first time is always the hardest. And you did it on the first try."

Ti An beamed with pride.

"Jodi, your turn," said Patrick. I went to the chalk bin and dipped my hands in the chalk. I was sure that I could do it better than Ti An had just done it. I'm stronger than Ti An, and I don't have her fear.

"It's all in the timing," Patrick said to me as I stood in front of the bars. "You've got to do the switch just before you reach the top of the bar, not at the top. If you're already at the high point of your circle, you're too late. Got it?"

"Got it," I said. I jumped onto the lower bar

and patted the high bar with chalk, trying not to miss a spot. I didn't want to fall off just because I was in a hurry.

Then I stepped back on the mats and grabbed the lower bar. I swung up in my routine. I did a clean glide kip, much better than I had done in the meet. I had my confidence back. I could feel the bars bend with the pressure of my swings.

I rebounded up to the high bar and began my giant backward circle. I concentrated on keeping my toes pointed and my elbows straight. I had so much momentum and power going around that I was over the bar before I could let go and try to cross my arms.

I got my body turned partway around, but I developed too much downward momentum. The bar was nowhere near where my hands could regrab it.

I was falling fast. Patrick grabbed me before I could hit the mats.

I had flubbed it. Patrick lowered me to the mats.

"I told you — you've got to time the release for the moment before you're at the top. Otherwise gravity will pull you down faster than you want."

I nodded. "Yup," I said. "Let me try it again."

"We'll give the others a chance," said Patrick. "But next time, concentrate."

I blinked. Patrick sounded annoyed with me.

I went to the bench and got my towel to wipe up the perspiration. Heidi and Dimitri were talking with their backs to me. I knew they didn't realize I was there.

"Ti An is really improving," said Heidi.

Dimitri grunted his agreement. "Yah," said Dimitri, "she's a little bug."

We had all learned that "little bug" is Dimitri's idea of a compliment.

"Jodi's good, too," said Heidi. "She's just so flaky."

"Flaky?" said Dimitri. Sometimes Dimitri doesn't get American slang.

"Sometimes she's great. Other times she just flops all over the place, like at their last meet."

I didn't know what to do. I didn't want the two of them to know I was eavesdropping.

"Patrick vill have to do vot's best for the Pinecones," said Dimitri.

I slunk away. I didn't want to hear any more. "Vot's best for the Pinecones" could turn out to be rotten for me.

5

A Little Like Living with a Tiger

The rest of practice was *not* a disaster. I didn't have any major flubs or goof-offs. Still I was happy to see practice end. Gymnastics is just not that much fun when you can't learn the new tricks.

I was the first one back into the locker room. I peeled off my tights and T-shirt and stepped into the shower. I turned the water as hot as I could and stood under it. I was happy standing there, with the water pounding my shoulders, letting my mind go blank. Some kids might think that my mind's a blank most of the time anyhow, but it isn't. Dimitri's comment really bothered me, and the worst thing was that I couldn't talk to anybody about it. If I talked about it I'd have to admit I had been eavesdropping.

It was much better to just stand in the shower.

"Hey, Jodi," I heard a voice say, "you'll turn into a prune."

I opened my eyes. Heidi was standing next to me in the shower. Heidi lathered herself up incredibly quickly and thoroughly. Then, in a blink of an eye, she was rinsed off and ready to get out of the shower. Heidi did nothing slowly.

No motion wasted. Heidi would never think of just standing in the shower and vegetating. That's probably why she's a world-class gymnast and I'm not.

I got out and put a towel around me. "I've got a favor to ask you," said Heidi, shaking her head and letting the excess water fly off her hair and face. Heidi is the only person I know who dries off from a shower like one of those TV commercials.

I dried the ends of my hair, trying not to show how surprised I was that Heidi would want to ask a favor of me.

The other Pinecones came piling into the shower. Heidi cocked her chin toward the corner of the locker room, to show me that she wanted to talk to me privately. I followed her into the corner, but I felt clueless. Heidi was much closer to Lauren or to Darlene than to me. If she needed something, she'd be much more likely to ask one of them than me.

"What's up?" I asked. "Do you want me to give you lessons in falling off the bars?"

Heidi didn't get it. "Why would I want to fall off the bars?" she asked.

I shook my head and twisted my hair to get the water out of it. "It was a joke, Heidi, just a joke. What's the favor?"

"My parents have to go to Europe for a couple of weeks, starting next week, and I need to stay with someone while they're away. Mom wanted me to stay with Darlene and her family, but I told her that I'd rather stay with you. But I thought I should check it out with you first, before my mother asks your mom."

Now I *really* felt clueless. Darlene and her family have a beautiful house with lots of land around it. We've got a new house, too, since Mom married Barney, but it's nowhere near as big or fancy as Darlene's.

"With me?" I blurted out. "Uh, Heidi, I don't think you realize our house has a few drawbacks."

"Oh, it's okay," said Heidi. "I'm not allergic to cats."

I wasn't thinking of my cat, Sar-Cat, whose name is short for sarcastic.

"I'm talking about Nick the Pest," I said to Heidi.

"Oh, he won't bother me," said Heidi. "He's kind of cute."

"Cute?" I repeated. "Heidi, he is not cute."

I still didn't get it. Heidi seemed dead set on staying with me, but the truth was that we weren't such good friends at all.

Well, it's not like me not to just come straight to the point. "Heidi, why me?" I asked. "It doesn't make sense."

"Oh, sure it does," said Heidi. "My mom didn't think it made sense at first, either, but it's because of your mom." She said it as if it were the most obvious answer in the world.

"My mom isn't your coach," I said.

"I know that," said Heidi impatiently. "That's what my mom said."

I didn't like being lumped together with Heidi's mom. She's always interfering in Heidi's life, and I know that Heidi and she don't get along. Heidi used to be anorexic and bulimic. In fact, when we first met her she was in the hospital. Several world-class gymnasts are borderline anorexic. That's never been my problem. I love to eat.

Heidi's mother has never liked the Evergreen Gymnastics Academy. She doesn't like Patrick. She barely tolerates Dimitri. To tell the truth, I don't know anybody who gets along with Mrs. Ferguson.

"Uh, if your mother doesn't want you to stay with us, maybe it's more trouble than it's worth."

"No," said Heidi fiercely.

"Why is it so important to stay with me?" I said.

"Not you," said Heidi, not even realizing she was being the slightest bit insulting. "Your mom. I figure there's a lot I can learn from her. She'll understand what I'm going through getting ready for the Olympics. It's important for me that I not lose an ounce of my momentum. I figured your mom can keep me focused."

I swallowed. I should have guessed that it didn't have anything to do with me.

"So, is it okay?" Heidi asked.

I shrugged. "Sure," I mumbled, "but I'll have to check with Mom and Barney, of course."

"Cool," said Heidi. "If it's okay with them, then that would be super." She turned her back on me as if that was all we really had to say to each other.

I walked over to my locker. Darlene had been glancing over at Heidi and me in the corner.

"What was that all about?" Darlene asked.

"Heidi wants to stay at our house while her parents are away," I said.

Darlene raised an eyebrow. "Yeah, yeah," I

muttered, "I would have thought she'd have stayed at your house."

"That's not what I'm surprised at," said Darlene. "I'm surprised you'd want her around twenty-four hours a day."

"Hey, Darlene, Heidi isn't Becky. I thought you liked her."

"I do like her," said Darlene. "I'm just not sure that I'd want to live with her. It would be a little like living with a tiger."

Darlene was the nicest and most easygoing person in the world. If she had second thoughts about living with Heidi, what had I gotten myself into?

6

I'm No Angel

Mom didn't say yes right away when I told her that Heidi wanted to stay with us a couple of weeks. She said that she wanted to think about it and talk it over with Barney.

Later that night at dinner, I brought it up again. "Why wouldn't it be okay?" I asked. "I want her to stay here." I wasn't absolutely sure about that, but I did know that I'd be very embarrassed if I had to tell Heidi no.

"Heidi can be pretty intense," said my mother.

"It'll only be for two weeks," I said.

"Do you really want her here?" asked Barney.

I shrugged. "I told you yes," I said. "Heidi says

that she wants to stay here because of Mom, not *me*," I said. "And I think it would be mean to say no."

Barney ladled out his spaghetti sauce. He's a much better cook than my mom, and he loves food. It shows, too. He's kind of fat. Heidi still has a tendency to be a picky eater. I wondered how she'd get along with Barney, who says that there are two kinds of people in the world: those who eat to live and those who live to eat. Barney is definitely one of those who lives to eat. He wakes up in the morning and can't wait to talk about what he's going to eat for dinner.

"I think it's neat that she wants to live here," said Nick. "She'll be like my sister."

"She will *not* be your sister, creep," I said.

Travis started to beat his spoon on his high chair. I shook my head. "I can't believe anybody wants to join *this* family!" I muttered.

"Jodi!" said my mother. "That's no way to talk."

"I'm sorry," I said quickly.

Nick grinned. He loved it when I got in trouble.

"This is your house, too, Jodi," said Barney. "You're the one who has to share a room with her. Your mom and I think you shouldn't be pressured into this."

"I don't think it's such a big deal." I could hear the whine in my voice.

"Your words are one thing," said Barney. "But I get the feeling that it's making you a little uncomfortable."

"Barney, please," I argued. "I've got a few other things to worry about right now besides Heidi. All the Pinecones are getting better than me. I'm really doing lousy."

Barney looked worried. "Jodi, if you've got so much on your mind, maybe having Heidi here isn't such a good idea."

"Oh, I'm sure she'll be a great inspiration!" I yelled. "Probably she'll be the daughter Mom always wanted. She's nearly perfect, like Jennifer, the squeaky-clean Air Force Cadet."

"Jodi!" said Mom. "Heidi is not the daughter I always wanted. You are."

"Only joking, Mom, only joking," I said quickly. I wanted *out* of this discussion. In fact, I wanted *out*, period.

"May I please be excused?" I said.

"What about dessert?" Barney asked. "I've got angel food cake with hot fudge sauce."

"I'm not hungry," I snapped. "Besides, nobody wants a fat gymnast. Heidi will remind everybody of that."

"Jodi," said Mom. "Heidi's eating habits were very unhealthy. She's worked very hard to overcome her illness. It's not anything to joke about."

34

I stood up at the table. "I'm sorry," I said. "Okay, I'm sorry for everything!"

I shoved back my chair without realizing that Sar-Cat was sitting underneath me. I heard a howl of protest as I stepped on poor Sar-Cat's tail.

He scampered out of my way. "Now I even owe an apology to the cat!" I fumed.

Nick laughed. Great, finally somebody was laughing at my jokes. Nick the Pest.

I passed my mom's room where all her trophies stood on a shelf. I closed the door to my room, being careful not to slam it. I knew Mom would be up there in a second if I slammed the door.

I sat down on my bed. I had twin beds for times that somebody slept over. I don't have a huge room. I wondered where Heidi was going to put her things. I just knew that she'd be incredibly neat and upset that my closet was such a mess.

I looked at the pile of clothes on the floor of my closet. I might as well hang them up.

I had started to clean my closet when I heard a scratching at my door.

I knew it was Sar-Cat, and I was glad. I really felt bad that I had hurt him, and I was worried that he would stay away from me for a long time. Cats can sulk, too.

I flung open my door.

Mom was standing with Sar-Cat in her arms.

I bit my lips. "That was a trick," I said, letting her in.

"I knew you'd let Sar-Cat in," said Mom. "I wasn't so sure about me."

Mom took a look around my room. "Cleaning up?" she asked, sounding surprised.

"Yeah, I'm not always a slob," I said, picking up a sweatshirt.

"You aren't a slob at all, Jodi," said Mom. "You're neater than your sister was at your age, or me for that matter."

I was surprised. I remember Jennifer as being extraordinarily neat.

"I hope Barney's not mad at me for not having dessert," I said to Mom.

Mom shook her head. "Actually, it wouldn't hurt Barney to go easy on desserts himself," she said. "I just wanted to come talk to you and find out what's got you so upset."

"I'm not upset," I said.

Mom looked at me. She knows when I'm not exactly telling the truth.

"I mean it," I protested. "Just chalk it up as one of those days. Everybody has one."

I took Sar-Cat out of Mom's hands and carried him over to my bed. He twitched his tail at me. I could tell he hadn't totally forgiven me for stepping on him.

36

"See? Even Sar-Cat's having a bad day," I said.

"You know, Jodi," said Mom, "Barney was right. This is your house, too. If you have any doubts about having Heidi move in, tell me about them. She'll have to share your bedroom. We don't have to have her."

"Mom, I *like* Heidi," I protested. "And it's only for a couple of weeks."

"I know," said Mom. "But I don't want anything to upset you."

"I'm not some fragile egg," I said. "It's me — Jodi — remember? I'm the daughter who bumps and falls and jumps right up again. I'm the original what-me-worry kid. Heidi being here is *not* going to be a problem."

Mom stood up. "Well, if you're sure," she said.

"She wants to come here because of you," I said to Mom. "That's what Heidi told me. She said that you knew what it was like to be a champion, what the pressure is like before the Olympics."

"I never made it to the Olympics," said Mom.

"But you would have if you hadn't gotten injured, right?" I said.

Mom shrugged. "I think so," she said. "I tore a ligament in my ankle, and that was before sports medicine was as highly developed as it is now. I was out for that whole season."

"And that's the year you married Dad," I said.

Mom smiled at me. "You don't miss a thing, do you, Jodi," she said. "Yes, that was the year I married your father. But I didn't marry him because I was disappointed in not going to the Olympics. . . . That wasn't the source of our problems. Your father and I had a number of great years together. And, most important, we got to share you and Jennifer."

"Right, Mom," I said. I had heard Mom's lecture about her and Dad's divorce about as many times as I had heard Patrick tell me to "turn the page." Mom always reminds me that both she and Dad love Jennifer and me — that their break-up had nothing to do with us or with gymnastics. It was all water under the bridge . . . et cetera, et cetera.

"Mom, I'm fine," I reassured her. "And having Heidi here will be a piece of cake."

Mom sighed. "I hope you're right. I'll call Mrs. Ferguson and work out the details. I'm sure she'll be worried."

"From what I know about her she worries too much," I said.

"She's a mother," said Mom, as if that explained everything.

I made a face.

Mom laughed. "Well, all right, Mrs. Ferguson can be difficult. I know that. Talking to her will not be a piece of cake. Anyhow, speaking of

pieces of cake, how about going down and join-
ing Barney and Nick? We don't want those boys
to eat the whole thing themselves, do we?"

I nodded. "Okay," I said. "The truth is that
even though I'm no angel, I love angel food cake."

"That's the Jodi I love," said Mom.

7

Nobody's in Awe Around Here

On Saturday morning, Heidi and her mother showed up at our house. I knew that Mrs. Ferguson had talked to Mom about all the arrangements. Barney answered the door.

"Hi ho, Heidi," said Barney. "What do you call a hen that's afraid to cross the road?"

"I don't know," said Heidi. She looked awkward. She was carrying a duffel bag. Her mother was carrying a very expensive-looking suitcase.

"Guess," said Barney. "Come on, I bet your mom knows. Hi, I'm Barney Josephson. Barking Barney." Barney held out his hand.

Mrs. Ferguson held on to her suitcase. She didn't shake Barney's hand.

"Chicken," said Barney.

"Excuse me?" said Mrs. Ferguson.

"That's what you call a hen that's afraid to cross the road," said Barney. "Here, let me take your suitcase."

"Hi, Heidi, Mrs. Ferguson," I said, welcoming them into the living room. Sar-Cat bounded across the sofa. The two hamsters, Itchy and Scratchy, rolled around the wheel in their cage. The hampsters were a recent addition. They were supposed to be Nick's pets, but he claimed they chased each other all night and kept him up when he tried to sleep. We've oiled their wheel, but they're still in the living room instead of in Nick's room.

"Where's your mother?" Mrs. Ferguson demanded of me. She didn't sound very friendly.

"Sarah's at the gym," said Barney. "But I wanted to be here to welcome Heidi. You know Barking Barney's motto: Everyone has room in their heart for a little love."

"Heidi is looking for a quiet place where she can concentrate on gymnastics," said Mrs. Ferguson. Heidi made a face.

"Oh," said Barney. "well, that's the motto of my store. I figure a pet brings a little love into every home. Heidi, I wasn't implying that you'll be a pet here."

Barney laughed. I thought Mrs. Ferguson was going to grab Heidi and make a beeline for the door. It seemed to me that Mrs. Ferguson thought Barney belonged in one of his pet stores himself — not as the owner, but in one of the cages. Barney is pretty hard not to like, but Mrs. Ferguson obviously thought he was a jerk. She made me mad.

"I'm afraid," sniffed Mrs. Ferguson, "that I've never been in one of your stores. I'm allergic to most animals."

"Heidi, how about you? Are you allergic to animals?" asked Barney.

Heidi shook her head. "No, I've never had one. I always travel too much to take care of one."

"Really," said Mrs. Ferguson, "the more I think about it, the more I realize that this will be just too much of an inconvenience for you and your wife, putting Heidi up. I should have thought of it before, with you working at your animal stores . . ."

"Pet stores," corrected Barney.

". . . and your wife busy at the gym," continued Mrs. Ferguson as though Barney hadn't spoken. "I'm afraid Heidi won't have the rest that she needs."

Barney looked at Heidi. "Heidi, you'll have to share a room with Jodi, but we're happy to have you."

"Thanks, Mr. Josephson," said Heidi. "I'd like to stay here if I still can." She glanced at her mother.

42

"Sure, only call me Barney. Jodi, why don't you take Heidi up and show her where to put her stuff?"

"Heidi," insisted Mrs. Ferguson. She coughed. "I think we'd better chat out in the car for a moment." The way she said "chat" made my skin crawl.

I already had Heidi's duffel bag. "Later, Mom," said Heidi, "after I get my stuff put away."

Heidi grabbed the suitcase and followed me up the stairs.

My room looked kind of small when I took Heidi up to it.

"I don't think your mother wants you to stay here," I said to her.

Heidi sank down on the bed and sighed. "Mom hates overweight people," she said. "I'm sorry she was so rude to your dad."

"He's my stepdad, not my dad," I said.

"I think he's cool," said Heidi.

My mouth dropped open. "Barney?!" I said.

Heidi nodded. "He's funny. I've been listening to his ads on the radio since I was a little girl."

Heidi dumped her stuff on the bed. I showed her a drawer I had emptied for her. She just shoved her things into the drawer without even bothering to sort them out.

"What about the suitcase?" I asked. "Don't you want to unpack it?"

"Nah," said Heidi. "Shove it under the bed. It's got a bunch of dresses and stuff that Mom insisted I take. I won't need them, will I? You guys don't dress for dinner."

"Well, we don't go naked," I said, giggling. "Remember, you'll be living with Nick the Pest."

Heidi laughed. "That's not what I meant. Mom makes me put on a dress for dinner."

"Every night?" I exclaimed. "Even when there's no company?"

Heidi nodded. "Mom says that it's European to dress for dinner, and if I'm going to be an international star I have to act like one. But I've met lots of European gymnasts, and they all say that they wear jeans to dinner."

"Weird," I said. "No wonder you weirded out over food."

Heidi laughed. "I've got to tell my shrink, Dr. Joe, you said that." She sighed. "I guess I'd better go downstairs and rescue your stepdad. Mom's probably giving him a hard time."

I got off the bed. "Heidi, why did you want to come here? Was is just to annoy your mom?"

Heidi looked shocked. "No," she said. "I really did think your mom could help me. And I like you, too. It's okay, isn't it?"

"Sure," I said quickly.

It was okay. And Heidi telling me that she liked me — that made me feel good.

44

It was funny. I have a reputation for being direct and honest, but Heidi just blurts out what she's thinking. It's as if Heidi hates to waste time with chitchat.

"Heidi, is there something going on here that I don't know about?" I asked her.

She stared at me. "Jodi, I've got a mother that bums me out, I've got the Olympic trials coming up — something I've worked for all my life — I don't have time right now for *anything* else."

"Yeah, I know," I said. "But — "

"Look," said Heidi. "Things will be fine once my mother leaves. Then you and I can both get back to gymnastics — that's what's important, right?"

"Right," I said. "But . . . but . . ."

"No buts," said Heidi. "Trust me on this. I just needed a place to stay where the *O* word wouldn't scare everybody."

"The *O* word?" I repeated.

"Olympics," said Heidi. "Everybody, including my own mom, is in awe of them. I knew that this was one house where nobody's in awe of anything, right?"

"Right," I said. "Nobody's in awe around here." I guess now was not the time to admit to Heidi that I *was* in awe of her.

8

A Lonely Hug

Mrs. Ferguson was sitting on the edge of the couch when we went downstairs. Barney was in his easy chair with his feet up. "I told your mother that some people say I'm a little like a fish," said Barney.

"Why's that?" asked Heidi.

"Because I don't know when to shut my mouth," said Barney.

I couldn't help laughing. Mrs. Ferguson gave me a dirty look as if she couldn't imagine why I would think Barney was funny. Well, who cared what she thought. Barney was definitely A-OK in my book. I'd rather have him as a stepfather than have Mrs. Ferguson as my mother any day.

"Heidi," said her mother, "I still would like to talk to you alone."

"I'm staying here, Mom," said Heidi. "I'm all unpacked."

Mrs. Ferguson sighed and got up. "I've given Mr. Josephson all the numbers where we can be reached, plus emergency numbers if there's any problem. You can call me day or night."

"Yes, Mom," said Heidi obediently. She gave me a wink.

Suddenly the door burst open, and Nick pushed into the room with three of his friends from the Atomic Amazons' gym.

"See?" said Nick, proudly. "I told you she was staying at our house."

"Nick," said Barney, "mind your manners." Nick actually does have manners when he needs them. He pulled up short when he realized Heidi's mother was in the room.

"Whoops, sorry," he said. He held out his hand to shake hands, the way Barney had taught him to do with grown-ups.

Mrs. Ferguson didn't look like she wanted to shake Nick's hand any more than she did Barney's. Maybe it was because Nick is a little overweight, too.

"This is my son," said Barney. "Nick, this is Mrs. Ferguson, Heidi's mother. My boy takes gymnastics at the Atomic Amazons' gym."

"Oh," said Mrs. Ferguson. "Darrell Miller is a very fine coach."

Heidi rolled her eyes. We all knew that Heidi's mother had wanted Heidi to work out at the Atomic Amazons' gym because it was more prestigious than the Evergreen gym.

Mrs. Ferguson seemed to look at Nick with more respect.

"You're Heidi Ferguson," said Rob, one of Nick's friends. "He told us you were here, but we didn't believe him."

"You knew she lived in Denver, dodo," said Charlie, another of the Atomic Amazons.

"In fact, I was at your meet on Saturday," said Heidi.

"You were!" exclaimed Charlie. "I didn't recognize you."

"That's because I was sitting with the Evergreen team," said Heidi.

"Oh, you must be friends with Becky Dyson, the one that won, huh?" said Charlie.

Heidi glanced at me. "No, actually I cheer for the level-six team, the Pinecones."

"The Pinecones," hooted Charlie. "They lost by a mile. They lose all the time."

"Not all the time," I muttered.

"I'm an honorary Pinecone," said Heidi. "Believe me, they won't lose next time. The next meet will be at the Evergreen gym. The Pinecones will have the home-gym advantage."

"You're not competing in the meet against our girls' team, are you?" asked Rob.

"No," said Heidi. "I compete in the elite division. But I'll be there. And the Pinecones have some surprises up their sleeves."

"Heidi," I hissed, "don't promise them something we can't deliver."

"It doesn't hurt to have them worried about you," whispered Heidi.

Heidi is always looking for that extra edge. Mrs. Ferguson stood up. "Heidi, I really do have to be going. Why don't you walk me to the car to say good-bye?"

Heidi jumped up.

Barney stood up. "Don't worry about a thing, Mrs. Ferguson," he said. "She'll be as safe with us as a bug in a rug."

"Why did the bug sleep in the rug?" asked Nick.

"That sounds like a Barking Barney riddle," said Charlie.

"I don't know," I said.

"Because it was sleepy," he answered, giggling.

"That's not a riddle. It's just stupid," I said. I hoped Nick didn't end up taking over the pet store business. He'd be terrible at making up jokes.

I watched as Heidi walked her mother out to her car. Her mom drove a fancy foreign car. Probably you needed to be dressed up to be able to drive in it.

Heidi and her mother were talking, but it looked as if Mrs. Ferguson was doing all the talking and Heidi had to do all the listening.

Then Heidi gave her mother a hug. They didn't really touch. There was lots of space between them. It was kind of a lonely hug. It made me feel sorry for Heidi. I never thought I'd feel sorry for her. I always thought it would be the other way around.

9

The Yoke's on Me

It was strange waking up in the morning and having Heidi in the room. It had been almost a week, and I still wasn't used to it.

"Did you sleep all right?" I asked her.

Heidi nodded. "I can sleep anywhere," she said. She got up and went to the shower. Her clothes from last night were all over the room. I picked them up and put them on the bed.

We went downstairs for breakfast. Heidi didn't make her bed. I wondered if she never had to make her bed in her own house. I'd made it for her — I really didn't mind. She was the guest, and I hated having our room look like such a pigsty.

Heidi doesn't talk too much in the morning.

We had breakfast. Heidi ate as much as me. She had cereal, bananas, milk, and a muffin. She certainly wasn't starving herself anymore.

Every day Mom drove Heidi to the gym after they dropped me off at school. While she was getting ready for the Olympics Heidi was taking all her classes through a correspondence school so she could concentrate on her training. It felt strange watching Heidi and my mom drive off together, as if they were coworkers, which I guess they were.

"What's it like having Heidi as a roommate?" asked Cindi.

"It's a little weird," I admitted.

"Why?" Lauren asked.

I shook my head. "Heidi makes me look like a neat freak," I said. "She's really messy. I never expected that."

Lauren stared at me.

"I know, I know," I said quickly. "I have a reputation for being kind of an airhead and a slob."

"Nobody calls you an airhead," said Cindi.

"Or a slob," said Lauren.

We went into class. I thought about Cindi's and Lauren's comments. They said it so matter-of-factly, as if it would never have occurred to them.

Lauren's mom drove us to the gym after school.

When we got there, Patrick was talking to Dimitri. The others went into the locker room. I looked around for Heidi to say hello to her. She was sitting on a bench, writing in a notebook.

I went over to her. "Hi, roomie," I said. "How's it going?"

"Get into your gear," said Heidi. "You shouldn't be out here."

I looked at the clock. We still had fifteen minutes until the start of the session.

"I'm fine," I said.

"Get moving," said Heidi, and she cocked her chin toward Patrick and Dimitri. "It never hurts to show them you're the first one off the starting blocks."

"It's not a race," I said. "This is just a practice."

"Jodi," said Heidi, "trust me on this. Get moving."

I shrugged. I went into the locker room and got changed.

Ti An was already in her leotard. "You're so lucky to have Heidi living with you," she said. "I bet she gives you lots of good advice about gymnastics."

"Yeah, she told me to get to practice on time," I muttered as I struggled into my leotard. I got it all twisted and had to start over.

"Why does a leotard always act like chewing

gum when you're in a hurry?" I said.

"I don't know," said Ti An. "But I bet it's a good riddle."

Ti An waited for me to come up with the answer. I finally got the leg holes straightened out and got into my leotard.

"It wasn't a riddle, Ti An," I said. "It wasn't even a joke."

"Oh," said Ti An, looking disappointed.

"So what advice *is* Heidi giving you?" Ti An insisted.

"Ti An," I said, feeling exasperated, "the only reason Heidi's staying with me is that she wants some of my mom's medals to rub off on her."

"Heidi's got so many medals of her own," said Ti An. "If she wants to rub the medals, she can rub her own."

"*That* was a joke, a little joke, Ti An," I said with a sigh.

"I get it," said Ti An. "Maybe Heidi will rub off on you."

"Yeah, right," I said. "Knowing my luck, I'll pick up the only bad habit she has — not making her bed."

"I don't think that will help in gymnastics," said Ti An. Her eyes were shining.

"Hey, Ti An, that's pretty funny," I admitted.

Ti An blushed. "Nobody ever thinks I'm funny," she moaned.

I put my arm around her. "I'll testify that you can tell a joke," I said.

"Nobody will ever be as funny as you," said Darlene.

"What am I?" I asked. "The official jokester of the Pinecones?"

"Yes," said Darlene, chortling. I could tell she was teasing me. But the truth was that everybody always did expect me to come up with a joke.

We walked out into the gym together.

Patrick blew his whistle. We went over to stand around him.

"I think it's vor the gu-u-ud of everybody," said Dimitri as he looked down at what Patrick had written on his clipboard.

"Thanks, Dimitri," said Patrick. "It helps to have your input."

"Good input — great output!" exploded Dimitri. Dimitri loves to make what he thinks of as American jokes. "A yoke, right?" he said. "Next veek the Pinecones show the Amazons what vor, right?" he said. He looked down at Patrick's clipboard again. "Here, I show you something," said Dimitri.

He took Patrick aside to talk to him.

"Let's hear it, Pinecones," I shouted. "Ve show the Amazons vot's for! No more yoke on the face for the Pinecones." I raised my right fist into the air. I thought about how cocky Nick's friends had been, saying the Pinecones always lose.

"Jodi, don't be sarcastic," whispered Lauren. "It's not nice. Dimitri's being serious. He really wants us to win. You'll only cause trouble."

I stared at Lauren. I couldn't believe that she thought I was being sarcastic. "I vant to vin," I protested. "I'm being serious."

"Oh, yeah," said Cindi with a laugh. "*You* being gung ho — give me a break."

"Don't you think we can beat the Amazons?" I asked.

"Well, yes," said Cindi, but she sounded doubtful. I wondered if she had been planning on adding a sentence: "We'll never beat the Amazons as long as you stay in your slump."

I sighed. I guess I was the wrong person to get all gung ho. The yoke was on me.

Clown of the Pinecones

Patrick came back from talking to Dimitri. "I've worked out the lineup for our meet next week," he said. "I've decided that we have to do something to shake ourselves up."

"We could try hanging upside down from the rafters," I said, not able to resist the wisecrack.

"This isn't a joke, Jodi," said Patrick. "I know you've been in a slump lately. It happens to all athletes. Sometimes you just have to wait it out, until you get your rhythm back."

"I know I'll do better at the next meet," I said to Patrick. I was serious. I did have a good feeling about the upcoming meet. Heidi was right. We'd have the home-gym advantage. My mom had always said that if you can't win at home, you can't win anywhere. Maybe Heidi's spirit would rub off on me. Heidi never let anything bother her; she focused on what was most important: winning.

"I'm sure you will," said Patrick. "That's why I'm taking the pressure off you. I'm putting Ti An ahead of you on the uneven bars. That way, the judges will probably give Ti An and Cindi higher scores. It's for the good of the team."

There was dead silence among the Pinecones. I could feel them all looking at me. I tried to keep my face from showing any emotion. But I knew that I was turning bright red. My face felt as if it were on fire.

I swallowed. I don't know why, but I had never expected this. I knew I had been in a slump. I knew everybody knew it, but I didn't expect that things would change because of it. I was so stupid. I couldn't believe it.

"It's nothing against you, Jodi," Patrick tried to explain. "It's just that Ti An has been so consistent lately. It's better for the whole team."

I shrugged. "Sure," I said.

"I'll probably fall off the bars," said Ti An. She giggled nervously.

I didn't dare look at her. I didn't dare admit how much I *wanted* her to fall off the bars.

"Okay," said Patrick, "let's get to work. We have a lot of things to work on if we want to try to catch the Amazons."

58

We went over the floor routine about half a dozen times, but my heart wasn't in it. I kept making stupid mistakes. I'd do my tumbling run fine, and then at the last minute, I'd step out-of-bounds.

"No, no, no, Jodi," said Patrick. "When you land a routine, take a breath. That breath should go right down to your feet. Your feet should feel like they have roots into the mats."

"Now you want me to be a turnip," I teased.

Patrick frowned. I guess he didn't think I was funny. Making jokes was my way of telling everybody that being demoted didn't hurt. I would die before I'd let anybody know how lousy I felt inside.

"Hey, Jodi," whispered Ti An as we moved from the floor to the uneven bars, "you're not mad at me, are you?"

"No, Ti An, I'm not mad at you," I lied. I knew it wasn't her fault that I had been demoted.

"I think Patrick should have given you some warning," whispered Darlene.

"What was he going to say?" protested Lauren. " 'Jodi, I've got some bad news for you'? It's a proven fact that it's easier to hear bad news right away."

"Yeah," I said. "Think of the ways Patrick could have done it. He could have said, 'Okay, Pine-cones, everybody who's feeling good today, raise your hand.' Then I would have put up my hand. 'Not so fast, Jodi.' "

"That's not funny," said Ti An.

"Forget it," I said.

"Jodi," said Darlene, "I don't blame you for being bummed out because of Ti An getting promoted."

"Would somebody who's bummed out do this?" I asked. I pulled back my hair and wiggled my ears. Not everybody could do it.

The Pinecones giggled.

Patrick blew his whistle. "Girls," he warned. "Could somebody let me in on the joke?"

"It's just Jodi," said Ashley. "She's clowning around."

Patrick sighed. "Now what, Jodi?" he said.

"Nothing," I said. "I was just getting my ears ready."

"Ready for what?" Patrick asked, the perfect straight man.

"For the wiggling contest," I said, making my ears wiggle up and down. "I'm going to pin those Atomic Amazons' ears back. They're going to be dazzled by my wiggling ears. My ears will get a ten."

Patrick was shaking his head.

"Oh," I said. "You mean ear wiggling is not a gymnastic event?"

Darlene was laughing uneasily.

Patrick put his arm around me. "Enough jokes. Show me what you can do on the bars."

I went to the chalk bin and dipped my hands in. Then I had an idea. I raised my hand. "Patrick, I've got to go to the bathroom."

Patrick shook his head. I knew he thought I was stalling, but what could he say?

He nodded. I scooped up a handful of chalk and took it into the bathroom. I looked at myself in the mirror. I was the clown of the Pinecones. At least I could be a really outstanding clown. I put the chalk on my ears and face. Then I got some lipstick and rubbed it on my nose and made myself a big wide grinning clown's mouth. Laughing on the outside, crying on the inside. Isn't that what they always say about clowns?

I went back out into the gym.

"Jodi?" exclaimed Patrick, staring at my face.

"I'm the clown on the uneven bars," I said. "I want to do something to make the judges remember me."

The Pinecones weren't laughing. I saw Heidi and Dimitri staring at me from the sidelines.

I blinked. I realized that I was on the edge of losing control.

I waited for Patrick to yell at me. He always yells when I go too far, and I knew I had gone way too far this time.

But Patrick just shook his head. "Don't ever

try a stunt like that at one of the meets, or again, for that matter. However, let's not waste any more time. Get up on the uneven bars." He didn't sound really angry at all.

I could feel myself turning even more red behind the chalk dust on my face. I would have felt so much better if Patrick *had* yelled at me. Did he really think I was just a clown?

I pretended I was a monkey and scratched under my arms. Lauren and Cindi started laughing.

"That's enough, Jodi," warned Patrick. I stopped, but the Pinecones couldn't stop giggling, and even Patrick didn't sound really mad. I guess I knew my place. I was the Pinecone clown.

11

Nothing More
Important
Than Being Honest

I went into the locker room after practice and quickly showered off all the chalk dust. I changed into my street clothes as fast as I could. I really wasn't in the mood for much more joking around. I had just had it with being the "funny one."

Heidi and Mom were waiting for me. I climbed into the backseat, letting Heidi sit in the front with Mom. Luckily Mom had been outside with the parents of the tiny tots during my clown exhibition. She hadn't seen it. I knew she wouldn't have approved.

Mom turned around before she started the car. "Jodi?" she asked me. She was staring at my hair.

"What?" I asked, knowing that I sounded annoyed.

"Your hair . . . what did you do to it?"

"Nothing," I said. "Let's go home."

Mom reached behind the seat and touched my hair. "It looks streaked," she said. "For a moment there I thought you had gone and dyed it, so you'd be a platinum blonde."

"That's not platinum. That's chalk dust," said Heidi, only she didn't sound as if she were making a joke.

"Yeah, it's the latest style in gymnastic accessories," I said. "Chalk dust in your hair. Everybody's doing it."

"That's not true, " said Heidi. "You're the only one doing it."

"Chalk dust?" asked Mom.

"Yeah, I was just clowning around," I said.

"Clowning around or being the clown?" said Heidi. "There's a difference."

"Heidi, I've already got a big sister, remember?" I said.

I stared out the window as we drove. Mom kept her eyes on the road, but Heidi twisted around to look at me.

"I know you must feel bummed out about Ti An," said Heidi.

"If I hear anybody else say that word one more

time, I really will be bummed out," I said.

"What's happened with Ti An?" asked Mom.

"Didn't Patrick post it where everybody could see it?" I said."I'm sure he told you."

"Patrick is going to use Ti An in front of Jodi for the next meet," explained Heidi. "That's why Jodi's in a lousy mood."

"Patrick didn't tell me," said Mom. "He keeps the running of the Pinecones to himself. After all, he's the one who has to live with the mistakes when he makes them. But changing the lineup doesn't mean that much. On my national team, we changed it for every meet."

"Sure, Mom," I said. I did not want to talk about this any longer.

In the front seat of the car were two champions — Mom and Heidi. In the backseat sat a chump. Mom occasionally tried to make me feel better by reminding me that she wasn't the best gymnast on the national team and that she never did get to perform in the Olympics, but right now the thought of my mom as a champion and me as a champion chump did not raise my spirits.

Nobody would ever call Heidi good at reading other people's moods. After we got home she simply would not stop talking about how I "must feel."

She followed me upstairs to my room. "I'm sure

if you work at it you can get your number-two position back."

I didn't answer her. Sar-Cat was curled up on Heidi's bed. Even Sar-Cat seemed to realize that Heidi was the star, but to be fair maybe it was just that Sar-Cat liked sleeping on Heidi's sweat-suit that she had left lying on her bed after breakfast.

Heidi picked up Sar-Cat and cuddled him. "I love cats," she said. "My mom's so allergic, I never thought I liked them, but I like Sar-Cat."

"He likes you, too," I said, grateful that we were off the subject of my demotion. I sat down at my desk and pretended that I had to do a lot of home-work. I opened my book, but I had actually done my homework in study hall. Anyone who knows me would be shocked.

Heidi just wouldn't stop talking. "You know what I think?" she said. Nobody ever asks that as a real question.

I kept my head down, pretending to be reading. Heidi didn't take that as a sign that I didn't want to know what she thought, however. She just barreled on.

"I think you should use this to make yourself go harder. It's not always a bad thing to have competition in a gym. It doesn't always mean trouble for a team. Mary Lou Retton once told me that when she was training at Karolyi's gym, he told her that it's important to have somebody pushing you. You can use Ti An as somebody to push you to be even better."

"Look, you and Mary Lou Retton and Mom are a different breed of cat," I said, taking Sar-Cat from Heidi's arms. I needed a cuddle myself.

"You can be honest with me," said Heidi. "I think there's nothing more important than being honest with yourself. I don't care how much you like Ti An — it's great when team-mates push each other, but you can't pretend you don't care."

"I'm not pretending," I said.

Heidi just looked at me.

"I'm not pretending anything," I protested. "Look — you are you. You *are* a different breed of cat from me." I looked down at Sar-Cat as if to emphasize the word *cat*. "I don't care whether I'm number one, two, or three."

Heidi just frowned at me. I was grateful when the phone rang and Nick yelled up the stairs, "Heidi, it's for you!" Barney had just bought us our first portable phone. Nick came bounding into the room with the phone in his hand. I knew that he would never have done that for me, but Nick had obviously gotten a crush on Heidi.

He handed the phone to Heidi. "It's long distance," he said. "Europe."

Heidi made a face. She took the phone. I started to leave and to shoo Nick out of the room so that Heidi would have some privacy.

"What, what?" whined Nick. "I was doing her a favor."

"I know," I said. "You were nice. Now, let her talk to her parents alone."

I got Nick out the door, when out of the corner of my eye I saw Heidi frantically waving at me to come back into the room.

I sat down on the corner of the bed.

"Hi, Mom," said Heidi. "How's your trip? No, no, everything's just fine here."

Heidi scrambled over to my desk and grabbed a piece of paper.

"Oh, good, good," she murmured into the phone. "Yes, I really am fine. Barking Barney is a great cook, and I'm eating very well. Dimitri and I are working on an added twist to my vault."

Furiously Heidi started writing something on the piece of paper she had grabbed. She handed it to me.

Call me for dinner! Please! she had written.

I raised an eyebrow. Heidi hadn't talked to her mother all week.

"Yes, I am taking my calcium," Heidi said.

"Look, everything is just fine here. Jodi and her mom are taking real good care of me. Jodi's mom drives me to the gym every morning. This is working out just fine."

I figured that if the phone conversation went on too much longer, Heidi would set a new world's record for repeating the word *fine*.

Heidi looked up at me, practically pleading with me. She kept pointing to the paper.

I licked my lips. Normally, it's not that I have so much trouble telling little "white lies." Still, this one was hard for me. However, I couldn't deny that Heidi was looking desperate.

"Heidi!" I shouted. "Dinner's on the table. It's hot!"

"Oh, Mom," said Heidi into the phone. "I've got to go. Barney's got a thing about everybody sitting down at the table together. I've *got* to go."

There was a pause on the phone as Heidi listened to her mother.

"Yeah, me, too," Heidi whispered into the phone. I wondered if her mother had said, "I love you," the way my mom did when she called me from far away. It sounded out of character for Mrs. Ferguson, but she was Heidi's mother, after all.

Heidi blinked. She looked about five years old. Then she pushed the off button.

"Nothing more important then being honest, huh?" I teased. Here Heidi had just been lecturing me on being honest, and she had been desperate for me to lie to get her off the phone.

I stared at Heidi. I couldn't believe it — Heidi Ferguson was wiping away a tear.

Allergic to Phone Calls

"Heidi?" I asked. "Are you okay?"

"Sure," said Heidi. She turned her back to me and rummaged under her bed for a box of tissues. She couldn't find it.

I gave her a tissue from the box on my desk. "Here," I said.

Heidi blew her nose. She made a very unladylike honk.

"Maybe I'm allergic to Sar-Cat after all," said Heidi.

"I don't think so," I said. "Heidi, you're allowed to be homesick."

"Oh, puh-leez," said Heidi. "You know what my mother's like. Would you miss her if she were away?"

"She's still your mother," I said.

"Look, Jodi," said Heidi. "I've got a shrink and two coaches. I don't need a friend to analyze me with my mom, okay?"

"Okay," I said. "but I still think you're allowed to miss your mom. I mean, she does care about you, maybe too much, but everything isn't always black and white. You don't have to be just one thing."

"Jodi," said Heidi, blowing her nose again, "believe me, I've got my mother covered. I know exactly how I feel about my mom." Heidi honked into the tissue again.

"That sound is really something," I said. "You'd better be careful not to do it around any Canadian geese. They might take you for their cousin."

Heidi laughed and then she sneezed. It was one of the loudest sneezes I had ever heard. It blew the papers on my desk off onto the floor.

I started to giggle.

Mom knocked on my door. "Jodi, Heidi, are you okay?" Mom asked. She slowly opened the door and peeked in.

We nodded, but every time Heidi and I looked at each other, we started laughing.

"What's so funny?" Mom asked.

"Nothing," I said. "Heidi just sneezed. She sounds like a goose."

"You aren't coming down with a cold, are you, Heidi?" Mom asked. She sounded worried.

Heidi shook her head. "No, I'm just allergic to phone calls from Europe," said Heidi. Somehow that joke surprised me. It didn't sound like Heidi. Maybe a sense of humor is catching.

"Did your mother call?" asked Mom. "I would have liked the chance to tell her how well things are going. I'm sure she's anxious being so far away."

"She's fine," said Heidi, using the same word that she had repeated so often to her mother. "She wanted to talk to you, but she had to hang up."

I looked at Heidi. I knew that was a lie, and somehow it didn't seem quite so funny anymore.

Mom looked a little confused. "Well, anyhow, girls, it's time for dinner. Why don't you come downstairs?"

"We will," I said. Mom went into Travis's room to see if he was awake.

"Why did you lie to my mom about your mom hanging up?" I asked Heidi.

Heidi shook her hand impatiently. "It wasn't an important lie," she said. "It didn't mean anything. Come on, I'm hungry."

Heidi hungry, Heidi telling "little white lies" — Heidi giggling, Heidi messy — there was a lot more to Heidi than I had ever guessed.

We went downstairs. Barney had made a special stew with pickles. He had even made the pickles himself. Barney likes to do everything from scratch. He not only loves to cook; he loves to experiment.

"So how go things at the gym?" asked Barney. "How are my high-flying girls? I tell you, Jodi, sometimes I look at the things you do at a meet, and I can't believe it. As for you, Heidi, what you do is absolutely inconceivable."

"No, it's not," said Mom, taking a bite of her stew and swallowing it. She paused. "This is delicious. Somebody who never cooked before wouldn't have the slightest idea how to put it together, but you started out learning how to boil an egg and then maybe, to make macaroni and cheese. It's the same with Jodi and Heidi. People see Heidi flying over the vault doing a double somersault in the air, and they think, 'I could never do that.' "

"Well, Mom, the truth is that I can't do what Heidi does," I argued.

"Maybe not yet," said Mom. "But look at what you can do. You started out as a little kid with a huge amount of energy who loved to jump on the couch."

"Did she get in trouble?" asked Nick.

"In our house jumping on the couch was considered the right thing to do," I said.

74

"Jodi always showed this tremendous energy. I didn't want to push her into gymnastics because I knew how hard it must be to come from a family where everyone was into it. In fact, I wanted her to do something else, but she just begged and begged to be allowed to go to the gym."

"I don't remember that," I said to Mom.

"You were only about three," said Mom. "You were littler than some of the tiniest tots I'm now working with at Patrick's gym. The point is, Barney, it's the same in all sports. When you see somebody doing something that looks incredible, you forget that they started learning the basics that don't seem scary. Nobody ever lets you aim higher until you're ready."

I took a bite of my stew and looked at my mom. I had forgotten that I had begged to go into gymnastics. I had always thought of myself as somebody who kind of got pushed into it.

"Mom?" I asked. "Did you mean that? You really didn't want me to be in gymnastics?"

"Your dad insisted that Jennifer do it. She was the older one, but by the time you were born, I had learned to speak my mind more, and I was determined that my younger daughter was not going to do anything she didn't want to. I've felt that way about each step you've taken. You've always surprised me by never wanting to stop."

Heidi was looking at me. "I knew there was something about Jodi that reminded me of myself."

I stared at Heidi, but Mom was nodding her head as if she agreed with her. Nick looked grossed out. "Oh, no," he said. "Heidi, I figured there was *nothing* about you that was like Jodi — that's why I liked you."

"You're wrong, Nick," said Mom. "Heidi and Jodi are quite a bit alike." She was smiling, but she was kind of serious. Maybe Heidi wasn't the only person who didn't know exactly how she felt about her mom.

13

No Clown Face Today

We had just three days before our next meet with the Atomic Amazons. I watched as Ti An worked on her bar routine.

She had added the one-hundred-and-eighty-degree turn to her routine, and it was clear she would be doing it at the meet.

The other Pinecones and I were sitting on some mats just to the side of the uneven bars, and we could hear every creak and groan as Ti An whipped around the high bar in her giant backward circle.

"She's gonna do it now!" said Lauren. We all watched intently as Ti An started to fall backward around the bar.

She let go and crossed her arms, causing her whole body to twist. She caught the bar with plenty of time to spare. "Good, Ti An, good," Patrick said.

Ti An finished her routine with a flourish. She smiled shyly at Patrick. She knew she had been good. I could tell it just in the way she moved.

Patrick signaled for Darlene to be the next up. Ti An sat down on the bench next to me and ripped off her hand grips. The pads of flesh underneath her fingers were bright red.

"My hands hurt today," said Ti An, gingerly touching the red spots.

"It didn't look it," I said. "You looked great."

"Thanks," said Ti An, "but I feel tired."

"Me, too," I said. "And my hands hurt, too."

Ti An nodded absentmindedly. I sneaked a look at her. I guess neither of us wanted to let the other know that we were after the same spot on the lineup. Ti An had won it — for now, but that didn't mean I didn't want it back.

I watched Darlene finish up her routine.

"I'm going to add that one-hundred-and-eighty-degree turn to my routine, too," I said to Ti An as I stood up.

Ti An looked at me. "Are you sure?" she asked. "It's hard."

"I know," I said.

"The last time you did it, didn't you fall?" asked Ti An.

78

"If you can do it, I can, too," I said.

Ti An laughed, sounding a little jittery.

"Jodi, what are you trying to prove?" asked Lauren, who had been listening to us. "It's not like you and Ti An are competing *against* each other. That would be bad for the team."

"I'm not trying to take anything away from Ti An," I said. "I just want to be the best that I can be."

"Whoo-eee!" teased Lauren. "Is this the new aggressive Jodi?"

" 'The best that I can be,' " joked Cindi. "It sounds like the army."

"I'm not kidding," I said, but it was clear that my teammates didn't believe me. They just couldn't see Jodi the Clown saying something like "the best that I can be."

"Jodi, you're next," said Patrick.

"Go for it," said Ti An.

I looked back at her. Ti An is not the type to be sarcastic or cute. But there was something about the way she said "go for it" that really bothered me, as if she didn't have to worry because she knew I'd never make it.

I walked over to where Patrick was waiting.

"Patrick," I said, "I want to add that one-eighty-degree turn to my routine for the meet next week."

Patrick shook his head. "Not yet, Jodi," he said. "It's too risky."

"You're letting Ti An do it," I said.

"Ti An's done it successfully in practice nine times out of ten," he said. "You've completed it only a couple of times."

"I can do it, Patrick," I said. "Let me put it in my routine right now. I know I'm ready."

He smiled at me. "Okay, Jodi," he said, "go for it!" When Patrick said it, it made me feel confident.

I went to the chalk bin where Heidi was dipping her hands in for a better grip on the vault.

"Any clown faces today?" Heidi asked me.

"No," I said.

"Ti An looked good on the bars," said Heidi.

"I know it," I said. "You don't have to remind me."

"Go for it," said Heidi.

"That's what everybody's saying," I mumbled.

Heidi gave me a look that seemed to say I shouldn't be joking around.

Patrick held me up to help me put more chalk on the upper bar. I could feel the butterflies in my stomach. I really didn't know if I could do the move half as well as Ti An did.

I clapped my hands carefully over the bin, shaking off the excess chalk. Then I walked back to Patrick. I was nervous.

"Remember," said Patrick, "the trick is in the timing. Don't rush it. You have much more time than you think you have to uncross your hands. The mistake comes when you try to do it too quickly."

I nodded my head. I just wanted to get on the bars and show everybody I could do it.

"Come on, Jodi," shouted Cindi. "Be all that you can be!" she giggled.

I shot her a dirty look. Cindi was my friend, and I knew she wasn't doing it to be mean, but I didn't like her making a joke just as I was about to start.

I ignored her.

I grabbed the lower bar and swung up into my routine. My swings had real power to them. I kept my leg muscles tight so that when I hit the lower bar, I bounced up tight, and the momentum carried me back over the top of the high bar with no problem. I was sailing. Then I reversed directions to begin the backward circle.

When I got to the height of the swing, I let go of the bar and uncrossed my arms. I grabbed for the bar, but my hands hit nothing but air. I had so much swing and speed that I didn't have time to break my fall. I fell down hard on my back on the thick mats beneath the bars.

The air whooshed out of me, and I couldn't breathe for a second.

Patrick rushed up to me. "Jodi?" he asked. "Are you okay?"

I tried to take a deep breath and get some air back into my lungs. I knew that I wasn't hurt; I just couldn't talk. It takes a lot of air to talk.

"Just lie there for a moment," said Patrick. "Get your breath back."

"As if I have a choice," I managed to gasp out. Patrick laughed. "Now I know you're okay. If you can make a joke, you're Jodi."

"Right," I said, pushing myself up. Ti An was staring at me. I knew she hadn't meant for me to see the look in her eyes. She was glad I was okay, but she was also glad I had failed.

14

Me First

I waited another minute and then slowly got up. My teammates started to clap for me. I took a mock bow.

Patrick still looked worried. I circled my head to get the cricks out of my neck. Everything was in working order.

"I'm fine," I said. I looked back up at the stupid bars. I couldn't believe I had missed my timing.

"Actually, you had too much height," said Patrick. "That was the problem. Go take a rest."

I went to get a drink of water. Heidi was sitting on the bench.

"Are you okay?" she asked me.

"Sure, you know clowns — we're made of rubber — we always bounce back."

"Cut that out," said Heidi.

I drew a finger across my throat and winked at Heidi.

"I mean it," said Heidi. "I've been watching. I saw what you tried to do. Don't quit."

"Heidi, in case you didn't notice, I didn't quit. The mats came up to meet me. I fell — hard."

"You were trying to do the same trick that Ti An's doing," said Heidi.

I shrugged. "Yeah, and Ti An can do it. I can't. It's that simple."

"Ha!" said Heidi.

" 'Ha'?" I repeated. "What does that mean, 'Ha'?"

"It's not simple. It's killing you that Patrick put Ti An ahead of you. You want to strangle the little thing."

"I like Ti An," I protested.

Heidi smiled. "Yeah, but that doesn't stop you from wanting to wring her neck for beating you. Face it, Jodi. You hate to lose."

"Loosey-goosey me?" I said.

"Don't pull that loosey-goosey stuff on me," said Heidi. "I've been your roommate. I can see what you're really like. Your friends think they really know you, but they don't have a clue. You're much more like your mother than you ever want to admit."

"Heidi, you're full of it," I said.

"I am?" said Heidi. "Okay, go back over there and tell Patrick that you're perfectly happy being third. Tell him you don't want to cause any trouble for the team. Tell him that you want to forget the release move."

Becky came up to get a drink of water. She looked down at me. "That was quite a fall you took," she said. "I guess you won't try that again soon. I don't blame you." Then she went back to the Needles who were working on their vaults.

Heidi rolled her eyes. Lauren had just finished her routine on the bars. I went back over to my teammates.

"What were you talking to Heidi about?" asked Ti An. "You two were so serious."

"She thinks I want to kill you," I teased Ti An.

Ti An laughed. "That's a joke, right?" she asked.

"Sounds like trouble to me," said Cindi.

"Maybe," I admitted. "Because I do want to do that release move again," I said. "I want to win back my number-two position."

"Give it a rest," said Cindi. "You've got plenty of time to learn that new move."

"Hey, Cindi," I said. "what makes you think that I don't want to be number one?"

Cindi giggled. "Oh, sure, Jodi. Is that a challenge?"

"Yes," I said seriously.

Cindi stared at me as if she weren't exactly sure whether to believe me or not. I didn't give her a chance to think. Maybe I was causing trouble on the team, but I didn't care. I had a right to try to beat Ti An, and even Cindi.

Patrick was chatting with Dimitri. They were moving the practice mats away from the bars. I looked up at the clock. It was five o'clock. We were finished for the day, except for our conditioning exercises.

I raised my hand and waved it in the air. Patrick saw me. "Jodi?" he asked. "You feeling okay from that fall?"

"I want to try that release move on the bars again," I said.

Patrick shook his head. "Not a good idea. You just took a bad fall. It's the end of the day. You're tired. You can try it next week."

"Next week will be after the meet," I argued. "I don't want to wait."

Patrick looked over at the mats where the Pinecones were sitting. Ti An and Cindi were listening to every word intently.

Patrick frowned. "I'm not going to change the order of the Pinecone team no matter what you do here today, Jodi," he said. "Ti An earned the number-two spot on the team."

"I know that," I conceded. "I just want the chance to try it again."

Becky and the Needles had come over to the bars. "It's our turn on the bars," whined Becky.

Patrick put up his hand. "One second, Becky. I want to give Jodi a chance to try this again."

Ti An jumped off the bench as if she had been pinched. "Hey," she shouted, not sounding at all like the little shy Ti An that I knew. "If Jodi can do it again, so can I."

She ran toward the bar.

"Me first," I yelled, reaching to grab the bars before she could get there.

Patrick put out his hands and held us both back.

"I asked first," I insisted.

"I'm the one who's going to be doing it in the meet next week," argued Ti An. "I need the practice more than Jodi."

Heidi was watching us.

"Jodi asked first, Ti An," said Patrick. "She goes first."

Ti An gave me a dirty look.

I turned my back and went to the chalk bin. The room had gone strangely silent around the uneven bars.

I took a deep breath and walked back to the center of the mats and stood under the bars.

Once again, Patrick held me up so that I could rub chalk dust on the upper bar. This time I was very careful not to leave any bald spots.

I took a moment to see myself doing the whole routine without a mistake.

I could hear a nervous titter over on the bench. Everybody was used to me just grabbing the bar and starting the routine as fast as I could. When I rushed I made mistakes.

I took my time. This time when I started to swing into my giant backward circle, I waited a split second longer to release the bar. I uncrossed my hands and kept my eyes on the bar. I grabbed it again. I could feel the momentum tearing at my fingers, but I kept my grip on the bar, and I had it.

I finished my routine with a perfect dismount.

"Good!" said Patrick.

"GUUUD!" Dimitri echoed.

A "guuud" from Dimitri was worth solid gold.

Cindi's and Ti An's hands were waving in the air. "Patrick, Patrick," they said. "We want to try it again, too. It's not fair that Jodi got a second chance."

For a second I felt badly. Maybe I was causing trouble on the team. My teammates and I had never really competed against each other before.

I wiped my face with my towel. And then I waved my hand in the air, too.

"Patrick," I shouted. "I want a chance to do it again, too."

Ti An bit her lip. "Not before me," she said.

15

At Least She Didn't Wish Me Bad Luck

On the day of the meet, I woke up early. I tried to pretend I was still asleep so that I wouldn't wake up Heidi. I pulled the covers over my head. Then I felt too hot, so I pushed the comforter down toward my feet, and it slithered off the bed.

I started to get cold, so I climbed down to the foot of the bed to get the comforter.

"Do you think you'll ever get it just right?" Heidi asked me.

I looked over at her bed. She was lying with her hands behind her back.

"What are you doing up?" I asked.

"Listening to you toss and turn, " said Heidi. She got out of bed and did some stretches.

Heidi did stretches morning, noon, and night.

"So you're nervous — that's a good sign. I'm always nervous before a meet. It's good luck."

I was about to protest and say I wasn't nervous, but I knew that was a lie.

I got out of bed and started to do my own stretches, something I never used to do outside of the gym. Heidi gave me a sidelong glance.

"What?" I asked.

"Nothing," she said.

Heidi and I did slow yogalike stretches for nearly forty-five minutes. Afterward I felt better, but I was still keyed up. All the yoga in the world didn't seem to calm my nerves today.

I could hear Mom and Barney talking downstairs, and then Nick was in the bathroom. He took a long time.

I banged on the door. "Hey," I shouted. "I've got a meet today. Would you mind not taking all weekend?"

"I just got here," Nick yelled back.

"No, you didn't," I shouted. "You've been in there for hours."

Mom came by carrying Travis. "What's the problem?" she asked.

"Nick won't get out of the bathroom," I complained.

Mom sighed. She knocked on the door. "Nick, speed it up a little, okay?"

Nick grunted.

I waited impatiently. Heidi came and stood outside the door in her bathrobe.

"I'm first," I said.

"Sure," said Heidi. "You don't have to snap my head off. I know all about nerves."

"I don't have nerves," I said. I banged on the door again.

"Right," said Heidi.

"Okay," I admitted, "I am nervous."

Finally Nick came out, and Heidi let me go in first. I took a shower. I wanted to stay under the hot water longer, but I knew then there'd be no hot water left for Heidi. I made it a quick one and let Heidi into the steamy bathroom.

"You shouldn't take too hot a shower," said Heidi. "It can sap your energy."

"I've got too much energy to sap," I snapped.

I got dressed and went downstairs. Barney and Mom were both sitting at the table. Travis was in his high chair.

"I thought I'd make you a special pancake breakfast today," said Barney.

"I'm not hungry," I said.

"Did I hear right?" Mom asked. "Did you say you didn't want pancakes for breakfast?"

"I'm too tense," I admitted.

"This isn't like you," said Mom. "You could

always eat before a meet. It forever amazed me. When I used to compete, I could never eat a bite before a meet."

Heidi came into the room. "I'm starved," she said.

Nick punched his forehead with his palm. "I don't believe it. Jodi-podi's not hungry, and Heidi-pidi wants pancakes."

"Nick!" I couldn't believe he'd say something like that. Nick knew that Heidi had been anorexic, and to make a joke like that was in disgusting taste.

Heidi shook her head. "It's okay," she said. "I like being teased about my eating habits. It shows nobody's scared about it anymore."

Barney put a plate of pancakes in front of Heidi. He looked at me.

"Are you sure you don't want any?" he asked.

"No," I said, pouring a little cereal into a bowl. "I'm really too wound up to eat."

"I thought you were Super Girl with nerves of steel," teased Nick.

"I'm glad Jodi's nervous," said Mom. "It's good."

I looked up at her. "Good?"

"It means that you care," said Mom. "I'm glad."

Just then the phone rang. Mom picked it up. "Oh, Mrs. Ferguson, I'm so glad you called. Heidi's doing splendidly. She's a terrific guest."

I looked over at Heidi, expecting to see her make a face, but she didn't.

"No, she's right here," said Mom. "We're having breakfast together. Here, I'll put her on."

Mom handed the phone to Heidi. "If you want to take it in the other room, you can," whispered Mom.

Heidi shook her head. She took the phone. "Hi, Mom," she said, sounding almost cheerful. "Yeah, I'm eating pancakes. Barney's a good cook. Jodi's got a meet today at the gym. I'm going to watch her."

Heidi was mostly silent while her mother said something. The rest of us kept eating, pretending we weren't listening. Nick finished his breakfast, plopped his dish into the sink, and took off. Mom decided that Travis needed changing and picked him up. Barney went back to the stove. I was the only one left at the table.

"Yeah, yeah," mumbled Heidi into the phone. I could tell the conversation was going downhill.

"Hey, Mom, it's Jodi that's got the meet today." Heidi listened a few more seconds and then handed the phone to me.

I shook my head. The last person I wanted to talk to at that moment was Heidi's mother. And I knew she didn't want to talk to me.

Heidi pushed the phone into my hand. I put it up to my ear.

"Uh, hello, Jodi," said Mrs. Ferguson in her clipped voice. I was right. She didn't sound any happier to be talking to me than I was talking to her.

"Uh, I'd like to wish you the best of luck today," said Mrs. Ferguson.

"Thank you," I said. I raised my eyebrows. I couldn't believe that Heidi was making me talk to her mother on the day of my meet.

"And thank you for making Heidi so welcome," Mrs. Ferguson continued. "She sounds like she's having a lovely time."

Mrs. Ferguson did not sound as if she approved of Heidi having such a good time. "Uh, it's okay," I stammered. "Here's Heidi. . . ."

I handed the phone back to Heidi. "Thanks, Mom," said Heidi softly into the phone. "I'll talk to you soon."

Mrs. Ferguson said a few more words. Then Heidi hung up. She looked almost cheerful.

I couldn't get over how different Heidi seemed from the last time she had talked to her mother.

She went back to eating her pancakes.

"That was weird," I said to Heidi. "Why did you make me talk to your mom?"

"It was Dr. Joe's idea," said Heidi.

I looked around the room. Heidi's shrink was definitely not in the room with us. "Your shrink said your mom should talk to me?" I asked. The whole idea gave me goose bumps.

Heidi giggled. "No, but I told him what you said to me about her still being my mother, even though most of the time she drives me crazy. He said you were smart, and he said that instead of letting her make me crazy, I should try to give her half a chance. I decided to try it."

"Well, at least she didn't wish me bad luck," I said, a little doubtfully.

"She isn't all bad," said Heidi. She played with her pancakes. "Dr. Joe says that caring isn't all bad, either. He said I shouldn't pretend that I don't care about my mother. That's just as bad as letting her rule my life."

I licked my lips. I thought about the meet coming up and realized that Heidi's words applied to me, too. I used to pretend I didn't care about winning or losing. Caring was making me nervous, but it also was making me feel alive.

16

Everybody Vins

I was the first Pinecone in the locker room. I changed into my official Evergreen leotard, the white one with the green pine tree on the chest. Cindi came in a few minutes later. "You're early," she said, sounding surprised.

"I wanted a little extra time to warm up," I said. Ti An, Lauren, Darlene, and Ashley all filed in. Each one of them seemed as surprised as Cindi to see me.

"Dressed already?" asked Ti An.

"Yup," I said.

"Is that 'yup' or a burp?" asked Lauren.

"It was yes," I said, not nibbling at the chance to make a joke.

"Hey, Jodi, loosen up," said Cindi, patting me on the back.

"I was loose at the last meet," I said, "and look what happened."

"So this time you really are going to 'dump the slump'?" asked Darlene.

"Yes," I said. I didn't feel like saying any more. Yes was enough. My teammates stared at me. I think they couldn't believe that I wasn't my old loosey-goosey self.

I went out onto the floor before everybody else and started my stretches. The Atomic Amazons were across the room. They hadn't even changed from their street clothes yet. I knew they were watching me, too, but I ignored them.

I stared into space as I slowly stretched my muscles, flexing my wrists to get the maximum rotation that I knew I would need on the bars. The other Pinecones came out and sat next to me. None of us made jokes.

Patrick came over to talk to us. "Girls, I like your attitude today," he said. "You look like you're all business — that's the way to keep the Amazons psyched out."

My heart was pounding, but I tried to act cool.

We finished our stretches. The Atomic Amazons kept giving us sidelong looks.

Patrick watched me as I finished my warm-ups on the beam. Then we went over to the bars.

I sighed. I *hated* the fact that Ti An was getting to do the new move and I wasn't. I knew Patrick didn't like to change anything on the day of the meet, but I figured it was worth a try.

"Please, Patrick," I begged. "Let me try doing the release move in the warm-up. If I do it then, you can let me put it in the meet."

"No," said Patrick. "Do the routine without the release move."

I frowned. It really bothered me that Patrick would let Ti An do it, but not me.

I knew enough not to fight him on the day of the meet. I did my routine without the new release move.

I landed my easier routine perfectly. Patrick patted me on the back.

"That was good," he said.

He signaled for Ti An to get ready for her warm-ups. She had her arms folded across her chest. She had been watching me warm up.

I knew she was happy that she was going to get to do the new release move and I wasn't.

Ti An went to the chalk bin and dipped in her hands.

Patrick had his arm around my shoulder. "Jodi, do you still want to put in the release move?" he asked me.

I couldn't believe he was giving me the chance.

"Yes," I practically shouted.

"But that's *my* move." argued Ti An.

"Shh," said Patrick. "It'll be a surprise for the

Amazons. They've been watching Jodi warm up. They won't be expecting it."

"You said Jodi wasn't ready," Ti An argued. She was glaring at me.

"I see something different in you today, Jodi," said Patrick. "Besides, I like the idea of hitting the Amazons with a surprise. But remember, if you get in the middle of the routine and feel shaky, take out the new move. Don't risk it. I'm depending on your judgment."

I was about to make a flip crack about who would depend on *my* judgment. But I didn't want Patrick to hear me say something like that. Patrick didn't have to know every little thing that I thought — every doubt. I nodded to show him that I understood.

"But, but, Patrick," stammered Ti An.

"Ti An," warned Patrick. "You're going to do just fine. If Jodi completes the move, the judges are bound to give you a higher score."

Ti An looked doubtful. She seemed to think that I was taking something away from her. I couldn't blame her. If I were in her place, I'd probably feel the same way.

It seemed to take hours to get the meet started. My stomach was doing its own flip-flops. Finally we got going. I thought my stomach would calm down once I got started, but I was still keyed up.

I did the best vault that I've done in a long

time. I scored high enough to push our team close to the top, but then Lauren faltered on her second vault, and we fell behind the Atomic Amazons.

Darlene took the beam and outscored all the Atomic Amazons.

Finally it was time for the uneven bars. I went to chalk up the high bar. Out of the corner of my eye, I could see Ti An watching me. I turned my head and realized that the Atomic Amazons were watching me, too.

Heidi came over to me. "Will you help me chalk the high bar?" I asked Cindi. "I don't want to get chalk all over myself this time."

"Let me do it," said Heidi. "It will give the Amazons something to worry about."

Heidi went to the chalk bin. She stood on the lower bar and very carefully and deliberately applied chalk to the high bar.

"Are you sure you're ready to do that move?" Ti An asked me.

"I'm going to do the rotation release," I said. "Same as you."

Ti An opened her mouth and then shut it. I knew she was feeling the pressure.

"Good luck," she said. I wondered if she meant it.

The Atomic Amazon who went before me was still waiting for her score.

I went back to the chalk bin to put some more on my hands. Patrick came over to me.

"Keep that focus," he said.

I was going to make a joke about falling on my face, but I swallowed it. I didn't really feel like joking.

I straightened my shoulders and saluted the judges. Heidi went to stand with Mom on the sidelines.

I grabbed the lower bar the way that I had hundreds of times. I pulled myself up and started my routine. I swung higher and higher, reminding myself to point my toes the way Dimitri kept drilling into Heidi.

I let go of the bar and swung away, uncrossing my hands and keeping my body stiff as a board as the momentum twisted me around, then I grabbed the bar. It started to slip out of my fingers, but I fought to keep hold of it.

I held on, just by my fingertips. I had to bend my arms to keep my grip, but I didn't fall off. I completed my routine with a solid dismount.

I saluted the judges. I could hear my teammates cheering, and Ti An was standing and clapping as loudly as anyone. I ran to the Pinecones.

"Great routine," said Cindi.

The Atomic Amazons were glaring at me. I am sure that they never expected the third-best

Pinecone to do that move. Well, I didn't intend on staying the third-best Pinecone for long.

"You were great," said Ti An, but I could tell she was tense.

"The bar's slippery," I warned her. "Be sure you put extra chalk on it."

"Thanks," said Ti An. She went to get ready to do her routine.

Heidi overheard me.

"Ti An's my teammate," I said, before she could say anything. "I want her to do well."

"I believe you," said Heidi.

I watched Ti An. To my surprise, I had told Heidi the truth. I did want Ti An to do well. We were Pinecones together. Ti An did great. But I'm not sure she was so much better than me. Nonetheless, the judges gave her a score a tenth of a point higher than mine. I knew that if I had gone second I would have gotten the higher score.

"How are you feeling, killer?" Heidi asked me.

"Grrr," I said, pretending to growl.

Heidi frowned. "I thought you weren't going to clown around anymore."

"Clowns can win, too," I answered

Heidi stared at me, but it was true. I didn't have to turn into Heidi Ferguson to be a winner. I would never take everything as seriously as Heidi does — that isn't my nature. But it didn't mean that I didn't want to be the best. I had inherited my mom's drive to win. Now I just had to prove it to the rest of the world.

Ti An came back to the bench. I stood up and held out my hand. "Way to go," I said.

Ti An was still breathing hard.

"Thanks," she gasped.

Dimitri and Patrick overheard us. "Ven teammates push — everybody vins!" said Dimitri.

Ti An and I glanced at each other. I think we both knew that Dimitri was right, and he was also wrong. Ti An wanted to keep her position. Only one of us could win.

The next meet wasn't for a month. I hoped I could win back my number-two position by then. More than hoped — I wanted it so badly I could taste it.

Heidi had said that I was more like my mother than I realized. I was more like Heidi than anybody knew. I didn't just hate to lose, I loved to win. Winning didn't mean that I couldn't still make jokes. But I could be fierce. I could be a fighter. I could be like Heidi and my mom — winners.

Everybody watch out. Jodi is coming into her own.

About the Author

Elizabeth Levy decided that the only way she could write about gymnastics was to try it herself. Besides taking classes she is involved with a group of young gymnasts near her home in New York City, and enjoys following their progress.

Elizabeth Levy's other Apple Paperbacks are *A Different Twist*, *The Computer That Said Steal Me*, and all the other books in THE GYMNASTS series.

She likes visiting schools to give talks and meet her readers. Kids love her presentation. Why? "I do a cartwheel!" says Levy. "At least I try to."

APPLE® PAPERBACKS

THE GYMNASTS™

by Elizabeth Levy

☐ MD44050-0	#1	The Beginners	$2.75
☐ MD44007-1	#2	First Meet	$2.75
☐ MD44049-7	#3	Nobody's Perfect	$2.75
☐ MD41565-4	#4	The Winner	$2.50
☐ MD42194-8	#5	Trouble in the Gym	$2.75
☐ MD42195-6	#6	Bad Break	$2.75
☐ MD42221-9	#7	Tumbling Ghosts	$2.75
☐ MD42820-9	#8	Captain of the Team	$2.75
☐ MD42821-7	#9	Crush on the Coach	$2.75
☐ MD42822-5	#10	Boys in the Gym	$2.75
☐ MD42823-3	#11	Mystery at the Meet	$2.75
☐ MD42824-1	#12	Out of Control	$2.75
☐ MD42825-X	#13	First Date	$2.75
☐ MD43832-8	#14	World Class Gymnast	$2.75
☐ MD43833-6	#15	Nasty Competition	$2.75
☐ MD43834-4	#16	Fear of Falling	$2.75
☐ MD43835-2	#17	Gymnast Commandos	$2.75
☐ MD44695-9	#18	The New Coach?	$2.75
☐ MD44694-0	#19	Tough at the Top	$2.75
☐ MD44693-2	#20	The Gymnasts' Gift	$2.75
☐ MD45252-5	#21	Team Trouble	$2.75

Available wherever you buy books, or use this order form.

Scholastic Inc., P.O. Box 7502, 2931 East McCarty Street, Jefferson City, MO 65102

Please send me the books I have checked above. I am enclosing $_____ (please add $2.00 to cover shipping and handling). Send check or money order — no cash or C.O.D.s please.

Name _____

Address _____

City _____ State/Zip _____

Please allow four to six weeks for delivery. Offer good in the U.S. only. Sorry, mail orders are not available to residents of Canada. Prices subject to change.

GYM891